W9-AAP-043

TO LEAH & NAOMI

LOVE UNCLES MATT + MATT FRIENDSGIVING 2022!

Copyright © 2022 Warner Bros. Entertainment Inc.
FRIENDS and all related characters and elements © & ™ Warner Bros. Entertainment Inc.
WB SHIELD: ™ & © WBEI. (s22)
SUPERGIRL and all related characters and elements © & ™ DC.

All rights reserved. Published by Scholastic Inc. *Publishers since 1920.*
SCHOLASTIC and associated logos are trademarks and/or registered trademarks of Scholastic Inc.

The publisher does not have any control over and does not assume any responsibility for author or third-party websites or their content.

No part of this publication may be reproduced, stored in a retrieval system, or transmitted in any form or by any means, electronic, mechanical, photocopying, recording, or otherwise, without written permission of the publisher. For information regarding permission, write to Scholastic Inc., Attention: Permissions Department, 557 Broadway, New York, NY 10012.

This book is a work of fiction. Names, characters, places, and incidents are either the product of the author's imagination or are used fictitiously, and any resemblance to actual persons, living or dead, business establishments, events, or locales is entirely coincidental.

ISBN 978-1-338-84043-8

10 9 8 7 6 5 4 3 2 1   22 23 24 25 26
Printed in China   62
First printing 2022

Art by Keiron Ward for Artful Doodlers Ltd.
Book Design by Yaffa Jaskoll

HOLIDAYS ARE BETTER WITH
F·R·I·E·N·D·S
THE TELEVISION SERIES

By Micol Ostow

Scholastic Inc.

Friends love to celebrate.

When it comes to celebrations, everyone has a special place at the table.

THE TRADITIONS . . .

DRESSING UP

TRICK
OR
TREAT!

A THANKSGIVING FEAST

LIGHTING CANDLES

COUNTING DOWN TO MIDNIGHT

TEN...NINE...EIGHT...

THE FOOD . . .

christmas ham (preferably **not** stolen!).

Turkey—don't forget your extra-stretchy pants!

Holiday cookies . . . and other treats!

Even mac and cheese!

THE MUSIC . . .

THE GIFTS . . .

FROM: PHOEBE
TO: JOEY

FROM: MONICA
TO: CHANDLER

FROM: ROSS
TO: RACHEL

FROM: JOEY AND CHANDLER
TO: ROSS

COLA DRINK

LEMON LIME

On **Halloween**, we dress up in costumes, and trick or treat.

Costumes can
be super.

Costumes can be soft
and fuzzy.

I'M SPUD-NIK!

Costumes can even be . . .
kind of confusing?

Thanksgiving is a time to gather and show gratitude for our loved ones.

We eat lots of different types of delicious food.
(But maybe stay away from the trifle?)

And remember: The turkey goes on the table,
not your head!

On Christmas, we decorate trees.

We give gifts, and we gather with our loved ones.

We even remember those less fortunate.

On **Hanukkah**, we light the menorah
for eight nights.

On New Year's Eve, we stay up until midnight!

HAPPY NEW YEAR!

Some people make New Year's resolutions—
goals for the coming year.

Learn to play guitar.

No more gossiping.

Do one new thing
every day.

Take more
photographs!

Valentine's Day is a celebration of love and friendship.

I LOVE YOU THIS MUCH!

(But remember, Ross, don't go overboard!
It's the thought that counts.)

It's never a bad idea to spend
time with friends!

Birthdays are a special little holiday just for you!

Sometimes your friends throw you parties.

Sometimes they take you out to a special dinner.

However you celebrate your big day, friends always make it more fun!

Friends know not every
celebration always goes smoothly.

And things don't go quite as you planned.

From family feuds,

to party-crashing pets,

from slightly silly squabbles,

to unexpected mistakes,

your friends are always there for
you when it's time to celebrate.

Sometimes they're grumpy, and not in the most festive mood.

But even when the heat is really on,

your friends are always ready to cheer for you,

and never fail to make celebrations unique!

Think about the friends who make
your holidays special!

Do you love
their special
secret recipes?

Would you carry
them home if their
feet hurt?

Of course!
That's what friends are for.

So, whatever you celebrate
when the holiday season is here,

JUST REMEMBER, IT'S
BETTER WITH FRIENDS.